ماما وهبه
والغول

Mamy Wata and the monster

written and illustrated
by Véronique Tadjo

Arabic translation
by Ahmed Al-Hamdi

MILET

كان ياما كان في قديم الزمان،
وسالف الأعصر والأوان،
كانت هناك ماما وهبه ملكة كافة المياه،
كانت تعيش بمفردها في مملكتها.
وقضت أيامها
تعوم في البحر،
وتلعب في شلالات المياه
وتسبح في الأنهار.

A long time ago,
a very long time ago,
Mamy Wata, the queen of all waters,
lived alone in her kingdom.
She spent her days
diving in the sea,
playing in the waterfalls
and swimming in the rivers.

كانت ماما وهبه
كريمة جداً.
وقد سمحت للحيوانات تشرب
من مائها
ودعت الرجال
يصطادون الأسماك أينما أرادوا.

Mamy Wata
was very generous.
She let animals drink
her water and
men could also fish
wherever they wanted to.

ولكن في يوم ما، حين كانت ماما وهبه
تسبح بأمن وسلام
في نهر فيه كثير من الأسماك الكبيرة
جاء شخص ما ليحذرها
أنه على مسافة مجرد أميال قليلة من ذلك النهر،
كان هناك غولٌ مرعبٌ
وكان يرعب الناس
في القرى المحيطة.

But one day, as Mamy Wata
was swimming peacefully
in a river with many big fish,
somebody came to warn her
that just a few miles away,
a horrible monster
was terrorising the people
of the surrounding villages.

كان الغول يعيش في الماء
وكان يأكل اللحوم.
وكان له وجه بشع،
وله عين واحدة في منتصف جبهته
وبضعة صفوف من الأسنان الحادة جداً.
وكان يضطجع منتظراً
ليثب على أي أحد
يقترب من النهر.

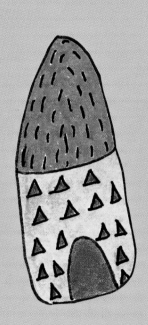

The monster lived in water
and was carnivorous.
He had a hideous face,
an eye in the middle of his forehead
and several rows of very sharp teeth.
He would lie in wait
and leap on anyone
who came close to the river.

وكان قد ابتلع اثنين
من صيادي الأسماك
كانا ينشران شباكهما،
كما ابتلع ثلاث شابات
جئن ليملأن جرارهن بالماء
وكثيراً من الأطفال
الذين أرادوا السباحة.

كان القرويون في حالة من اليأس.

He had already swallowed
two fishermen
who were casting their nets,
three young women
who came to fill their pots
and lots of children
who wanted to swim.

The villagers were desperate.

قررت ما ما وهبه
أن تذهب وترى
ما بامكانها أن تقوم به في أمر الغول.

وقد اطلعت على الكهف
حيث كان يأوي الغول فيه
للنوم في الليل.
فأنزلقت الى داخل الكهف
واخفت نفسها في زواية منه.
وعندما جاء الغول
ودخل في الكهف،
أخذت تراقبه.

Mamy Wata
decided to go and see
what she could do about it.

She was shown the cave
where the monster
went to bed at night.
She slipped in
and hid in a corner.
When the monster
came in,
she watched him.

لم يتمكن الغول
أن يغفو بسهولة.
فأخذ يُعوّلُ كثيراً
ويصدرُ كَثيراً من الضجيج
أثناء تنفسه.
ثم أهتز
جسده برمته.
وتفجرت الدموع من عينه.
ولكن بعد فترة، هدأ روعه
وصار يغط في نوم عميق.

The monster could not
fall asleep easily.
He moaned a lot
and made all sorts of noises
while breathing.
Then his body
shook all over.
He burst into tears.
But after a while, he calmed down
and fell into a deep sleep.

لمست دموع الغول
قلب ماما وهبه الطيب.
وغمرتها الرأفة عليه.
وعندما حان الصباح،
سحبت نفسها بهدوء مقتربة منه.
فربتت على ظهره برفق
وهمست بكلمات حنونة،
فاستيقظ الغول وهو يبتسم
وأخبر ماما وهبه بسوء الطالع الذى جرى عليه.
وكان في الحقيقة رجلاً شاباً
ولكن قد حولته احدى الساحرات الشريرات
الى غول
لأنه رفض أن يتزوج إحدى ابنتيها.

The monster's tears
touched Mamy Wata's heart.
She was filled with pity.
When morning came,
she quietly drew close to him.
She stroked him gently,
whispering kind words.
He woke up smiling
and told her of his misfortune.
He was in fact a young man
who had been turned into a monster
by a wicked witch
because he had refused to marry
one of her daughters.

أدركت ماما وهبه
أن الغول كان
حزيناً جداً.
وقررت أن تجعله
سعيداً مرة أخرى.
فاخترعت ألعاباً جديدة له.
وعلمته كيف يغني.
وعلمته كيف يرقص.

كان الغول مسروراً للغاية
لأنه وجد صديقاً
حتى أنه انفجر ضاحكاً.

Mamy Wata realised
the monster was
very sad.
She decided to
make him happy again.
She invented new games for him.
She taught him how to sing.
She taught him how to dance.

The monster was so delighted
to have a friend
that he burst out laughing.

وفجأة،
وبينما كان لايزال غارقاً في الضحك،
لاحظت ماما وهبه
أنه قد تغير تماماً.
وتحول الى رجل شاب
كما كان من قبل!

وفي نفس الوقت،
ظهر الصيادان،
والشابات الثلاث،
وكافة الأطفال الذين
ابتلعهم عندما كان غولاً
وعادوا جميعاً الى أهلهم
بأمن وسلامة.

All of a sudden,
while he was still laughing,
Mamy Wata saw
he had changed completely.
He had become the young man
he was before!

At the same time,
the two fishermen,
the three young women,
and all the children
he had swallowed up
reappeared and went back home
safe and sound.

أراد الشاب
أن يعيش مع ماما وهبه الى الأبد.
وأقاما معاً احتفالاً كبيراً
دعيا فيه كافة الناس
حول المياه.
وفي القرى،
فرح الجميع فرحاً غامراً.
وزينوا الأكواخ بالألوان الزاهية
وصارت القوارب
تتراقص في النهر.

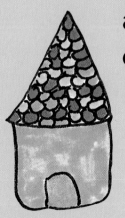

The young man wanted
to live with Mamy Wata forever.
Together, they held a big party
to which all the people
of the water were invited.
In the villages,
everybody rejoiced.
The huts were decorated
and beautiful boats
danced down the river.

Other Véronique Tadjo titles by Milet:

The lucky grain of corn
Grandma Nana

Milet Publishing Ltd
PO Box 9916
London W14 0GS
England
Email: orders@milet.com
Website: www.milet.com

Mamy Wata and the monster / English – Arabic

First published in Great Britain by Milet Publishing Ltd in 2000
© Véronique Tadjo 2000
© Milet Publishing Ltd for English – Arabic 2000

ISBN 1 84059 264 8

We would like to thank Nouvelles Editions Ivoiriennes for the kind permission
to publish this dual language edition.

Designed by Catherine Tidnam and Mariette Jackson
Printed and bound in Belgium by Proost